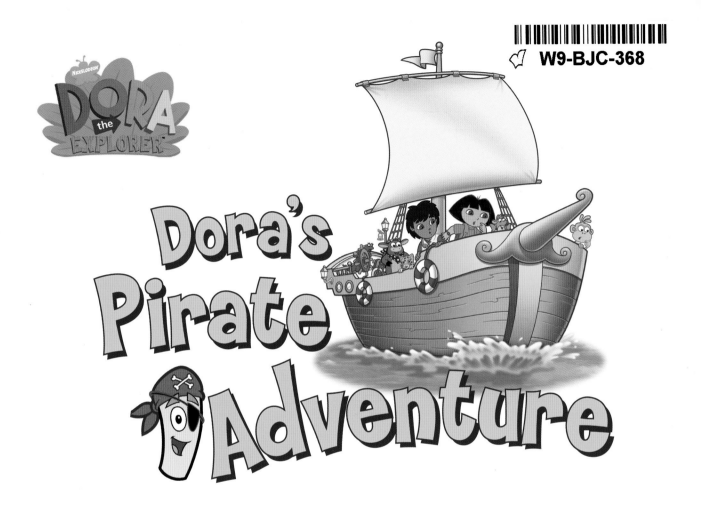

Dora's Pirate Adventure

adapted by Leslie Valdes
based on the original teleplay by Chris Gifford
illustrated by Dave Aikins

SIMON AND SCHUSTER/NICKELODEON

Based on the TV series *Dora the Explorer* as seen on Nick Jr.

Simon and Schuster
First published in Great Britain in 2006 by Simon & Schuster UK Ltd
1st Floor, 222 Gray's Inn Road, London WC1X 8HB
Originally published in the USA in 2005 by Simon Spotlight,
an imprint of Simon & Schuster Children's Division, New York.
© 2005 Viacom International Inc. All rights reserved.
NICKELODEON, Nick Jr., *Dora the Explorer*, and all related titles, logos
and characters are trademarks of Viacom International Inc.

A CIP catalogue record for this book is available from the British Library

ISBN 978-0-85707-427-0
Printed in China
10 9 8 7 6 5 4 3

Visit our websites: www.simonandschuster.co.uk
www.nick.co.uk

Ahoy, mateys! I'm Dora. Do you want to be in our pirate play? Great! Let's go and put on our costumes!

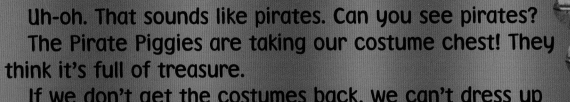

Uh-oh. That sounds like pirates. Can you see pirates?
The Pirate Piggies are taking our costume chest! They think it's full of treasure.

If we don't get the costumes back, we can't dress up like pirates. And if we can't dress up like pirates, then we can't put on our pirate play.

We can get our costumes back. We just have to know where to go. Who can we ask for help when we don't know where to go? The Map!

Map says the Pirate Piggies took the treasure chest to Treasure Island. We have to sail across the Seven Seas and go under the Singing Bridge, and that's how we'll get to Treasure Island.

Can you see the Seven Seas? Yeah, there they are! We can use that boat to sail across!

¡Fantástico! Now it's time to sail the Seven Seas. Let's count the Seven Seas together. *Uno, dos, tres, cuatro, cinco, seis, siete.*

Good counting!
Now we need to find the Singing Bridge. Where is the bridge?

Yeah, there it is. *¡Vámonos!*

We have to teach him the right words.
Let's sing the song the right way.

Row, row, row your boat,
Gently down the stream,
Merrily, merrily, merrily, merrily,
Life is but a dream!

Yay! We made it past the Singing Bridge! Next up is Treasure Island. Can you see Treasure Island? Yeah, there it is!

Look! There's a waterfall. Isa has to turn the wheel, or we'll go over the edge.

Uh-oh! The wheel is broken! Maybe Backpack has something that will help us. Quick, say "Backpack!"

We need something to fix the wheel. Can you see the sticky tape?
Yeah, there it is! *¡Muy bien!*

Turn the wheel, Isa!
Whew! We made it past the waterfall.
Come on! Let's go to Treasure Island, and get our costumes back!

We found Treasure Island. Now let's look for the treasure chest. We can use Diego's telescope

There it is! Come on, mateys, let's go and get our costumes back!

The Pirate Piggies say they won't give us back our treasure. We need your help. When I count to three, you need to say "Give us back our treasure!" Ready? One, two, three: Give us back our treasure!

It worked! *¡Muy bien!* The Pirate Piggies say we can have our treasure chest back!

Thanks for helping us get our costumes back. Now we can put on our pirate play. We did it! Hurray!